the Just Right Gift

A Story of Love

the Seven Teachings Stories

Katherena Vermette
Illustrated by Irene Kuziw

HIGHWATER PRESS

Migizi loves his Gookom.

He wants to get her a gift,
but it has to be just right.

He wants to find something
as sweet as her kisses
and as warm as her smiles.

Migizi goes to the store with his Mom.
He finds gold earrings that
sparkle in the light,

but they are not just right, and he doesn't have any money anyway.

He goes to the park
with his class.
He finds some big,
beautiful roses,
but they are not just right,
and Mr. Bee says you are not
supposed to pick those anyway.

Migizi wants to cook
a great, big moose roast –
Gookom's favourite –
but he doesn't know how to cook,
and his dad says it's not time
to hunt moose anyway.

He wants to make her
the best painting ever,
but he only has crayons.
His sister says his drawing is good,
but he just can't get it just right.

Nothing he can buy,
pick, make, or paint
is as sweet as Gookom's kisses
or as warm as her smiles.

And then he thinks of it –
the one thing she always asks for.
It's the one thing he can't buy,
pick, make, or paint,

the thing he does more
just right than anyone else.

So, the next time he visits,
he gives her a great
big, beautiful, sparkly
hug.

And it is as sweet as her kisses,
as warm as her smiles,
and it is just right
for both of them.